A Haights Cross Communications Company

Published by
Sundance Publishing
P.O. Box 1326
234 Taylor Street
Littleton, MA 01460
800-343-8204
www.sundancepub.com

Copyright © text and illustrations by Edizioni EL
Text adapted by Michele Order Litant and Wendy Benger

First published 1999 by
Edizioni EL
Via J. Ressel, 5
34147 San Dorligo della Valle (TS)
Italy

Exclusive North American Distribution: Sundance Publishing

ISBN 0-7608-6713-5

Printed in Canada

Anita
the Tree

Nicoletta Costa

sundance

A Haights Cross Communications Company

Anita the tree is a
good friend to everyone.
Her friends like Anita
for different reasons.

Anita gives Corky the cat
a place to climb up high.
Corky likes being able
to see far away.

Mrs. Blake likes hanging up her wash on a branch. The fresh air makes her wash smell good.

Anita gives Peggy
a place to swing
way up high.
Peggy likes feeling
as if she is flying.

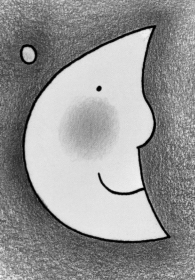

The owls like to play
on a branch at night.
Anita is sleeping, but
she does not mind.

Anita gives the birds a good place to practice their tricks. They like Anita's strong branch.

The birds like to sit
on Anita's branch
when it rains.

Her leaves keep them dry.

Anita gives Peggy and Ben
a place to practice climbing.
They like to see how high
up they can go.

In the fall, the birds like to play with Anita's leaves. Anita does not mind because her leaves are falling anyway.

But the birds fly away
when the leaves are
almost gone.

This makes Anita sad.

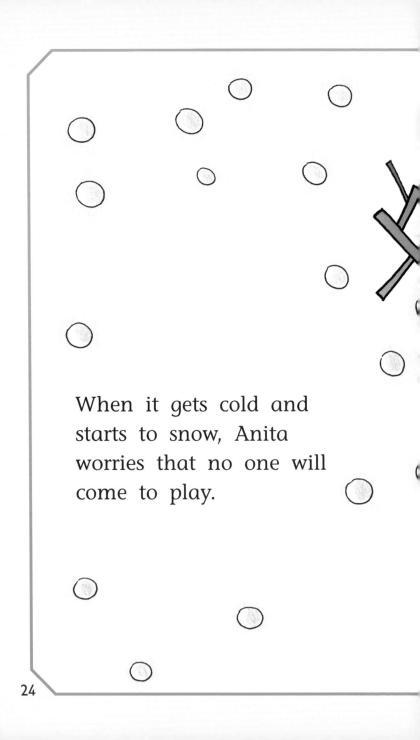

When it gets cold and starts to snow, Anita worries that no one will come to play.

But the children and Corky
the cat do come to play.
They like the snow, and
they like Anita!

Fun Pages

Have some fun with these puzzlers!

Look at each picture. How many things can you find that are different?

There are four things on these branches that don't belong. Can you find them?

SunLit Library

Set 1	Set 2
Anita the Tree	Alexander the Bat
Daisy and Tina	The Captain and the Whale
The Giraffe Family Vacation	Granny Vanilla Takes to the Sky
Granny Vanilla's Magic Cookies	Holly the Hoozeewhat
Moka All Year Round	Katy and the Telephone
Moka Delivers the Mail	The Lily Pad Olympics
Mole and Mouse	The Long Bus Ride
Mr. Kite Gets Stuck	Moka Above the Clouds
A New Friend	Nikki and the Ark
Nikki's Costume Party	Pedro the Painter
Scout Flies Away	Summer Adventure
Sunny's Red Spots	Super Cat to the Rescue

Here are some ideas for things to talk about.

☆ How is Anita a good friend to everyone?

☆ If you lived in Anita's neighborhood,

which of her friends would you

play with? Why?

☆ Pretend Anita could talk.

What might she say?

I would like to talk about _____